9.95

Do You Sing Twinkle?

A Story About Remarriage and New Family

by Sandra Levins
illustrated by Bryan Langdo

MAGINATION PRESS WASHINGTON, DC

American Psychological Association

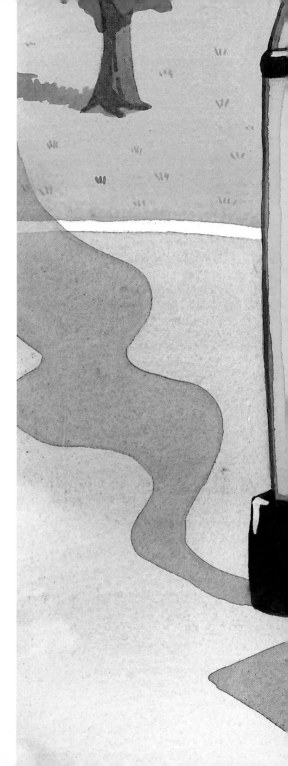

To my parents, Oran and Darline Wagler—SL

For Nikki, Oliver, and Harper, for filling my life with happiness—BL

Published by
MAGINATION PRESS
An Educational Publishing Foundation Book
American Psychological Association
750 First Street, NE
Washington, DC 20002

For more information about our books, including a complete catalog,
please write to us, call 1-800-374-2721, or visit our website at www.maginationpress.com.

Printed by Worzalla, Stevens Point, Wisconsin

Library of Congress Cataloging-in-Publication Data

Levins, Sandra.
Do you sing Twinkle? : a story about remarriage and new family /
by Sandra Levins ; illustrated by Bryan Langdo.
p. cm.
"American Psychological Association."
Summary: A boy's parents help him adjust to his new stepfamily
when his mother remarries after a divorce. Includes note to parents.
ISBN-13: 978-1-4338-0539-4 (hardcover : alk. paper)
ISBN-10: 1-4338-0539-1 (hardcover : alk. paper)
ISBN-13: 978-1-4338-0551-6 (pbk. : alk. paper)
ISBN-10: 1-4338-0551-0 (pbk. : alk. paper) [1. Divorce—Fiction.
2. Remarriage—Fiction. 3. Stepfamilies—Fiction.] I. Langdo, Bryan, ill. II. Title.

PZ7.L5792Do 2010
[E]—dc22   2009008609

10 9 8 7 6 5 4 3 2 1

For a long time, my brother and me lived with Dad part of the week and Mom part of the week.

We walked to school when we were at Dad's and rode the yellow school bus from Mom's house.

See, we have divorce in our family.

But that all changed when Mom married Tom and moved to Springfield. The school bus didn't go *that* far away! That's when we had to make a hard choice.

Hard choice is a grown-up word for choosing between two not-so-perfect things and dealing with it the best you can. So now we live with Dad all week, and we stay with Mom in Springfield every other weekend.

But that's not the only thing. Mom has a new family! She has a new husband, Tom, who is not my dad, and worst of all, new kids.

Girls!

Mom says Erin and Amy are my stepsisters now. And I am Erin and Amy's stepbrother.

Stepsister or *stepbrother* is the grown-up word for when your mom or dad marries somebody else who is not your dad or mom and that person has kids. If the kids are boys, they're stepbrothers. If the kids are girls, they're stepsisters. The new person your mom or dad marries is your stepdad or stepmom.

But I don't want stepsisters! Amy sits on my mom's lap, and Erin whines if she doesn't get her way. Everything is always about those girls. Princess movies, doll houses, tea parties. Yuk!

I have a brother and that's all I want!

Every Sunday night at the halfway point, Dad is waiting. Mom gives us hugs and kisses, and we buckle up in Dad's car. It is always past our bedtime when we get home.

We brush our teeth and then go straight to bed.
Dad tucks us in and kisses us goodnight.

We skip a story because it's too late.

Tonight I think about Mom. She always reads to us at bedtime. She tucks the blanket up to our chins and kisses our heads. Then she sings "Twinkle" to my brother and me.

I bet that now she
reads to those girls.
And tucks the blanket
up to their chins.
And kisses their heads.
And sings "Twinkle."

Mom shouldn't sing
"Twinkle" to anybody
but my brother and
me! I am not a baby,
but I start to cry.

In the morning Dad says, "You're kind of grumpy, Little Buddy. Are you tired?"

"A little," I mumble.

"Maybe we should get you home earlier on Mom Weekends."

"No, Dad! I'm fine," I say.

I am grumpy, but I don't want
to leave Springfield even sooner.

I yank my brother's arm.

"Come on! Let's go to school," I say.

"Have a good day. I love you guys," says Dad.

I do not have a good day.

I do not feel like reading so I say
"Pass" when it is my turn.

I shove my partner
at the drinking fountain.

I throw woodchips at a
first-grader on the playground.

I punch Zoey Enos in the arm.
My teacher calls my dad.

I'm in big trouble, mister!

At home Dad says, "Mrs. Curtis said you had a rough day. What's up, Little Buddy?"

My tummy does a somersault. I blurt, "I don't like it that Mom lives far away! I like her old house! I don't get to see her enough. And I don't like all those steps!"

Dad tries to hug me, but I push him away.
I run to my room and slam the door.
I kick my brother's blocks and throw
Blue Bunny against the wall. I cry and cry.
I am not a baby. I am mad!

Later, Dad peeks into my room. "Your mom is on the phone. She wants to talk to you."

"Hi, Mom," I say.

"Dad told me you had a rough day," says Mom. "I'm sorry about that."

Just like that, it all comes out.

"I don't think you have time for my brother and me anymore. Maybe you don't think about us. You live too far away. And I don't want stepsisters."

"Oh honey, I think about you all the time," says Mom. "I'm sorry we can't be together as often as we'd like, but I have some ideas that might help."

Mom tells me to watch for the mailman to bring something. Two days later we get a fat envelope with a chapter book for me and a picture book for my brother.

A note says,

"Call me when you get this. We'll read it together. Love, Mom"

Reading on the phone is almost as good
as having her right next to me.

Then a calendar comes in the mail from Mom. She circled all the days that we'll get to see each other.

A couple days later, Dad says we have e-mail from Mom.

The next day Dad drives my brother and me to the halfway point. Mom is there waiting for us. Alone. I am surprised. And happy. She gives great big hugs and says, "Oh, I missed you guys so much."

Then, just to me, she says, "Did you know that Uncle Ian is my stepbrother? At first, we didn't like each other at all. He put a sign on his bedroom door that said,

NO GIRLS ALLOWED!

And I didn't want to share my mom with him."

Then Mom explained about finding common ground. *Common ground* is the grown-up word for finding a way so that you both feel comfortable. You might find things that you both like to do, and you'll start to know each other better.

"Did you know Erin plays soccer?" says Mom.

"But what about bedtime?" I ask.
"Do you read to those girls?
And kiss their heads?
And sing 'Twinkle'?"

"Actually, bedtime is the quality
time they share with just their dad," says Mom.

Quality time is a grown-up word for the time
parents spend with kids to show that they
really love them. My brother and me get a lot of that.

"Honey, no one will ever replace you. You and your brother
will always be my boys. You always fill my heart with twinkles."

Mom squeezes us so tight my eyeballs might pop out!

"So, Mom? How about singing 'Twinkle' right now?"

Note to Parents

by Jane Annunziata, PsyD

Parental divorce is a major stress and challenge for children of any age. And if parents begin dating, remarry, or move across town or farther, the emotional challenges kids face significantly increase. Any changes in family structure and routines that follow can feel overwhelming and confusing. While it requires the support and guidance of both parents to help children work through difficult feelings, children can master this life change.

Helping Your Child With Post-Divorce Changes

When parents begin dating, move to new homes, or remarry, children may "relive" many of the initial distressing emotions they experienced when their parents separated and divorced. To help children tackle these post-divorce changes, parents should talk to their children about what is about to occur. Your approach should be simple and straightforward, and try to parcel out information in small kid-size bites and in sequential conversations. Don't overwhelm your child with all the possible scenarios and talk about each step only when you know for certain that it will happen.

Dating and Remarriage

The first post-divorce adjustment for kids is when one or both parents begin dating. You might prepare your child for this by saying, "Now that your mom and I are divorced, we will be making some new adult friends. I may want take some of these friends on a date. A date is when grown-ups go out together. Even though I will start dating, I'll always make sure that we have lots of time together just the two of us."

The next challenge for parents can be introducing remarriage. You might begin with, "Honey, you know I've been dating Tom for a long time now, and I really think he is a wonderful man. I've really come to love Tom, and he loves me, too. Of course, it's different than our special mother-daughter love that will always be just for you. Because we love each other, Tom and I have decided to get married. We know it's a big change for kids when their parents get married again, and we are going to help you with all the feelings you will have about this."

Parental remarriage involves your child becoming used to having a new parent. Follow your child's lead regarding how ready she is to feel close to her stepparent, how much time she wants to spend just with him, and what she wants to call him. Some children (especially younger ones and those who don't have a biological mom or dad available) are eager to call a new stepparent Mom or Dad; others are more comfortable just using the parent's first name.

Additionally, children are most likely to accept a new stepparent and have good relationships when you facilitate. Help your children find "common ground" with a stepparent by pointing out similar interests and doing simple bonding activities together like baking cookies or taking the dog out for a walk. Be careful when you facilitate these connections and do not push to make everyone a "big happy family" too quickly. Always follow your child's cues.

You might need to address anything that may be interfering with the development of a mutually satisfying relationship between your child and his stepparent. Two common factors that get in the way are: feeling disloyal to the biological parent and feeling angry at a stepparent for reprimands or discipline. If you think loyalty issues are getting in the way, sit down with your child and say, "I notice that you seem to like Tom and have fun with him, and then all of a sudden you don't want to talk to him or be with him much. Do you have any ideas why that might be?" If your child offers an idea, follow up on that first, of course. But if he has no idea why this occurs, or offers an idea that just doesn't seem plausible, raise the loyalty possibility. You can start by saying, "Sometimes kids feel bad when they have fun with their stepdad because they worry that they aren't being loyal to their own dads, or they worry that their dad would feel bad because they like the stepdad so much. Do you think you might be feeling something like this? Do you know that your dad is really glad that you are happy here with me and Tom, even though I know he misses you a lot?"

Generally, the discipline is best left primarily to biological parents whenever possible, as they have the closest relationship to the child. There are, of course, exceptions to this. There will be times when a child will actually better respond to feedback delivered by a stepparent or when the "parent on site" has to move in with an immediate consequence or comment that the child will experience as criticism. Just remember to use as much empathy as possible when you deliver your message. You might say, "I know it's hard to hear this, especially from a stepmom, but I can't let you speak to your little brother in that hurtful way."

Stepsiblings and Blended Families

Remarriage frequently involves stepbrothers and sisters, which adds another "layer" of potential conflict. The stress involved with stepsiblings is three fold. First, the child has to share her parent and watch Mom or Dad actively parent "someone else's kids." Sharing is rarely easy for kids (especially for younger ones). Watching Mom with a little one on her lap reading a story or having a good time with a stepchild can evoke feelings of anger and jealousy or even "sibling rivalry." Both sibling rivalry and sharing issues can actually be worse with a stepsibling. This is especially the case if: your child is your only child and now has to share you for the first time, perceives a special closeness between you and your stepchild, or senses that you feel particular pleasure in a stepchild's talents (this is especially hard if your child feels "lacking" in an area where her stepsibling excels).

Second, your child knows that your expectation is that she "get along with" her new stepsiblings. This is challenging because they have not grown up together, lack a common history, may be far apart in age, and may not have a natural affinity for each other.

Third, when parents remarry, the child becomes part of a new blended family (which often doesn't blend very well at first). When both parents remarry and step-children are involved with both remarriages, the child becomes a member of two new blended families. This is a lot for children to manage and can understandably feel overwhelming and confusing at times. You can facilitate your child's adjustment to this transition by giving him lots of support and time to become comfortable before these relationships become formalized by marriage.

Helping Your Child Cope

There are many techniques that parents can use to ease the way for children navigating two families post-divorce. Combine these techniques with your own unique knowl-edge of your child, and adjust them depending on your child's age and individual situation.

Recognize Your Child's Stress
While it's good to emphasize the positives in the experi-ence and maintain optimism that you will ultimately become a new (and happy) blended family, be careful not to minimize the difficulties and feelings that your child is experiencing. It is important to acknowledge the reality of the stresses involved for children when a parent remarries (especially when stepsiblings are involved). When parents minimize the "negatives," children tend to "embrace" them even more. You might say, "I can see that you are not feeling happy about me marrying Kate. It is upsetting to feel like you have been pushed to be a part of something that you don't want and wish wasn't happening. I would feel angry and stressed, too. But I also know that kids can work through these hard feelings, and I'm going to help you to do that. We will take our time so we can all feel more ready for this big change, and eventually things will feel okay again." If you think that something in particular is making it hard for your child to accept the idea of your remarriage, be sure to address it directly. Common factors that interfere for kids include: worries that the other parent will be jealous or depressed when their ex-spouse marries, worries that they will be displaced by the parent's new spouse, and feelings evoked by this powerful reminder that Mom and Dad will never be together again.

Allow and Encourage Expression of Feelings
Give your child room and permission to express the array of feelings and reactions that are inevitable with this new family arrangement. Children may feel angry about the loss of control when parents remarry and the new people and routines in their lives that might be unfa-miliar and feel uncomfortable (especially at first). Anger also arises from the loss of control inherent in the blended family situation. The child experiences this as, "No one asked me whether I wanted a new stepdad or stepbrother!" Anger also relates to feelings of jealousy about sharing Mom or Dad with a new husband or wife and sometimes stepchildren, too. Also, children can feel nervous about fitting in and being comfortable in their new blended family. They may worry about the unfamil-iar and different things like getting used to a new home in a new town (or in another part of their town), as well as new stepbrothers and stepsisters, a new stepparent, and new rules and routines.

Negative feelings are often particularly difficult for children to express, and your child may need you to "lead the way" by giving suggestions of how children some-times feel. For example, if you sense that your child is unhappy or angry but isn't saying it, you might say, "A lot of kids feel angry when a mom remarries (or moves out of town) and spends time with new stepchildren. Kids often don't like thinking about that. I wonder if you might sometimes feel that way?" Or "You looked angry and sad when Tom and I were talking about taking a va-cation alone together. Were you feeling that way? It's okay to tell me. I won't feel angry at you for saying it."

Also, give your child room to express positive feel-ings about his new family members. Reassurance that it's okay and perfectly "normal" to like the way his stepdad takes him bowling or to enjoy having a "big step-sister" goes a long way toward easing any loyalty concerns. Help your children understand that forming good relationships within their blended family does not take anything away from their feelings about or rela-tionship with their biological family members.

Additional Coping Techniques
The following ideas are especially helpful when manag-ing long distance custodial arrangements, but many of them are also useful and easily adapted to situations when Mom and Dad live near each other.

Sometimes remarriage leads to relocation. This involves even more feelings for kids and parents to manage. Relocation can exacerbate a child's negative reactions to a new stepparent ("You took my mom away from me!") and stepsiblings ("You get to spend more time with my mom than I do!"). Here are a few strategies to ease the stress involved in this situation.

Remind Your Children That You Miss Them
Be sure you tell your children how much you think about them and miss them when you are not together. Some-times children (especially younger ones) think they are "out of sight, out of mind" for their parents, which is never the case. Letting children know how close you feel to them even when there is a geographic distance can be very reassuring.

Giving your children a calendar to keep track of their visits can be helpful, too. Some parents like to use the same calendar at their house, so their children know that Mom or Dad is looking at the same calendar page. Cal-endars are, of course, also helpful to keep track of visits back and forth between Mom and Dad, even when they live in the same town. They are very organizing for chil-dren and give them a sense of control over a process that so often feels out of their control.

Communicating in different forms gives you more opportunities to let children know that you are thinking of them whether you live close by or further away. All children love to receive "real" mail—cards, postcards, and brief, simple notes in the mailbox can be a nice surprise and are a great way to connect, too. Cell phones, text messages, and e-mails are very popular with older children and facilitate your child responding to you, keeping the connection going both ways. Even a young child who can't yet read or type can be read an e-mail from a parent and helped to send a return e-mail. Computer web cams work, too. These video cam-eras enable parents and children not only to see each other, but they give children the opportunity to "show" their parent an exciting new purchase or a recently completed science project.

Keep Your Time Together Special
Making sure that you spend time alone with your chil-dren when they are visiting helps them feel more secure and ultimately better able to bond with their stepparent and stepsiblings. Along these lines, it is helpful to be

alone when the children are being dropped off by your ex-spouse for their visit. The drop-off location is often at a midway point, which can mean a long ride to your home. While this can be tiring for children, it provides you with an opportunity to transition and re-connect with them and address anything that may be bothering them. This segue time alone with Mom or Dad generally lays the groundwork for a more relaxed and successful visit for all.

Children have many, often inaccurate, ideas about the nature of a parent's relationship with stepchildren. It is not uncommon for them to imagine that you engage in "their" special routines, with their stepsiblings. This can be very upsetting! Make sure that you keep some routines and traditions just for them, and let them know that you are doing this.

Maintain a Sense of Belonging
Help your children recognize that although a major change is occurring in your life, your love for them will never change or be replaced. This helps children to accept that although you are living farther from them now, they will always be primary in your life. Keeping a favorite routine in place (albeit in a modified form), helps children and parents keep the connection especially when there is a geographic distance. Special songs

can be sung, books can be "read together," the sports page can be discussed over the phone. Let your child have some input about what this special routine might be.

Help your children become familiar and comfortable with the area where you live. Make sure they get to know the local parks, library, and shops. Something simple like having a library card helps them feel part of a community. Sometimes kids like to develop special routines when they visit Mom or Dad (e.g., going out for bagels on a Saturday morning at a favorite bakery). This not only helps them have something to look forward to, but also helps them feel more "at home" in your new community.

Help your children feel more "at home" during their visits by providing them with a bedroom that is just for them (if at all possible) and giving them a chance to decorate it with you. If your child needs to share a bedroom with her stepsibling when she visits, make sure she has something in that room that reflects her and her interests.

Looking Ahead
One of the most helpful and healing things that a parent can do in divorce and remarriage is to communicate positive thoughts and feelings about the other parent. This can be quite a large task, given that people generally

divorce because they are unhappy with each other. However, children benefit immensely from hearing good things about their mom from their dad and vice versa. Be honest, of course, and look for opportunities to say nice things. For example, if your child comes home from a weekend and says, "We had a fun barbeque at Mommy's house," you might reply, "I'm glad to hear that. Your mom is great at grilling out!"

Most children are able to reach a stage of resolution and acceptance regarding their new family arrangements with the help and support of their families. Remember that bonding and blending with new family members is a process that not only takes time, but develops over time. Make sure to share this perspective with your children, too. However, should you find that despite all your best efforts your child is having continued trouble adjusting to this major life change, it can be useful to seek consultation with a mental health professional.

Jane Annunziata, PsyD, is a clinical psychologist with a private practice for children and families in McLean, Virginia. She is also the author of many articles and books addressing the concerns of children and their parents including a Magination Press book, Sometimes I'm Scared, *co-authored by Marc Nemiroff.*

About the Author

Sandra Levins lives in Burlington, Iowa with her husband and two adolescent stepsons, the inspiration for her stories. As a remarried mom and stepparent, Sandra has seen the hurt and confusion that happens when kids share a parent with a new family. Her ever-growing family includes adult sons, daughters-in-law, and two precious grandchildren. She sings "Twinkle" to them all. Sandra is also the author of *Was It the Chocolate Pudding? A Story for Little Kids About Divorce.*

About the Illustrator

Bryan Langdo has illustrated nearly twenty books as well as various magazine spots. He spends his days with his kids, playing with cars, ___ TIPP CITY PUBLIC LIBRARY ___ ne science museum. He lives in a very old house in upstate N___ ___ two kids, Oliver and Harper.